One Dad
Two Dads
Brown Dad
Blue Dads

by
Johnny Valentine
illustrated by
Melody Sarecky

ALYSON
WONDERLAND
an imprint of Alyson Publications, Inc.

to Jacob,

who has only one mom and one dad

But don't feel sorry for him.
They're both pretty great parents.

Text copyright © 1994 by Johnny Valentine.
Illustrations copyright © 1994 by Melody Sarecky.
All rights reserved.
Typeset in the United States of America; printed in Hong Kong.

Published by Alyson Wonderland,
an imprint of Alyson Publications, Inc.,
40 Plympton Street, Boston, Massachusetts 02118.
Distributed in England by GMP Publishers, P.O. Box 247, London N17 9QR, England.

First edition: July 1994

5 4 3 2 1

ISBN 1-55583-253-9

One dad,

two dads.

Brown dad,

blue dads.

"Blue dads?
BLUE dads!?
I don't know who
has dads that are blue!"

"I do!
My name is Lou.
I have two dads
who both are blue.

They both have blue hair,
that's the color it grows.

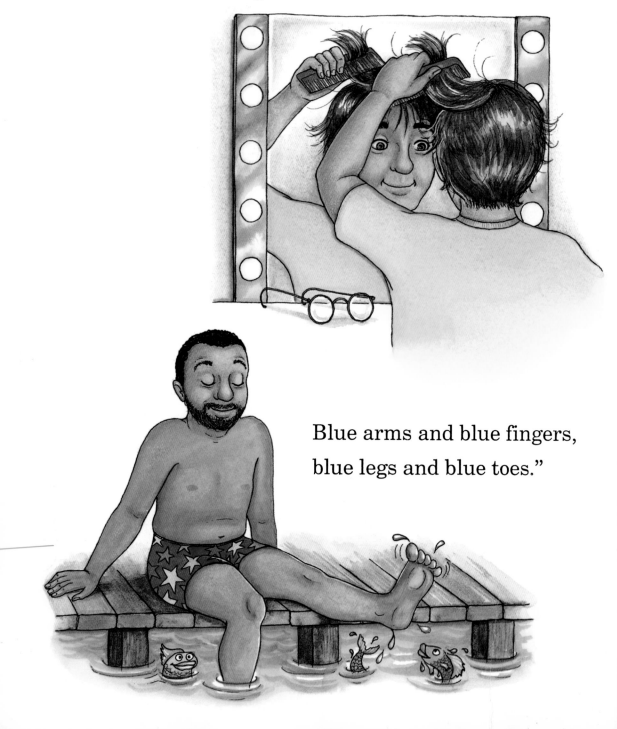

Blue arms and blue fingers,
blue legs and blue toes."

"What is it like to have blue dads?" I said.
"Do they talk? Do they sing?

And eat cookies in bed?

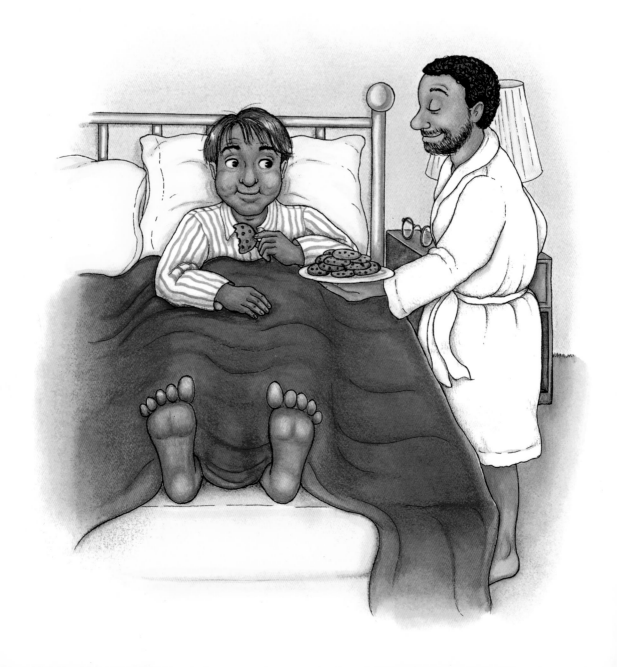

Do they work?

Do they play?

Do they cook?

Do they cough?

If they hug you too hard,
does the color rub off?"

"Of course blue dads work!
And they play and they laugh.
They do all of those things," said Lou.
"Did you think that they simply
would stop being dads,
just because they are blue?"

"My dad can stand on his head," I told Lou.
"My dad plays me songs on his purple kazoo.
He even knows how to make chocolate fondue!
Can blue dads do all those things too?"

"What funny ideas you have," replied Lou.
"Do you think dads are different,
because they are blue?
My dads both play piano,
and one of them cooks.
(He makes wonderful chocolate cream pies.)

I have never seen either one stand on his head.

But I'm sure they both could,

    . . . if the need should arise."

"What I'd like to know now,"
I went on to say,
"is: How did your dads
end up being this way?

Did they go through the wash
with a ball point pen?
Or were they both blue
since the young age of ten?

Did they drink too much
blueberry juice as young boys?
Or as kids, did they play
with too many blue toys?"

"Just where did you get all these questions!"
Lou said.
"How did *such* explanations
pop into your head?
They were blue when I got them
and blue they are still.
And it's not from a juice,
or a toy, or a pill.

They are blue because — well —
because they are blue.
And I think they're
remarkable wonders — don't you?

Yes, my dads both are blue.
And although you may try,
it is hard to see blue dads
against a blue sky.

But except for that problem,
our life is routine,
and they're just like all other dads —
black, white, or green."

"Green dads? GREEN dads!?
That I never have seen.
No, I never have seen
a dad who was green!"

"I have!
My name is Jean.
I have two dads
who both are green.

I'd love to let you take a look.

But we've run out of room now, in this little book."

Alyson Publications publishes a wide variety of books with gay and lesbian themes. For a free catalog or to be placed on our mailing list, please write to:

Alyson Publications

40 Plympton St.

Boston, MA 02118

Indicate whether you are interested in books for gay men, lesbians, or children with gay or lesbian parents.

ALYSON
WONDERLAND

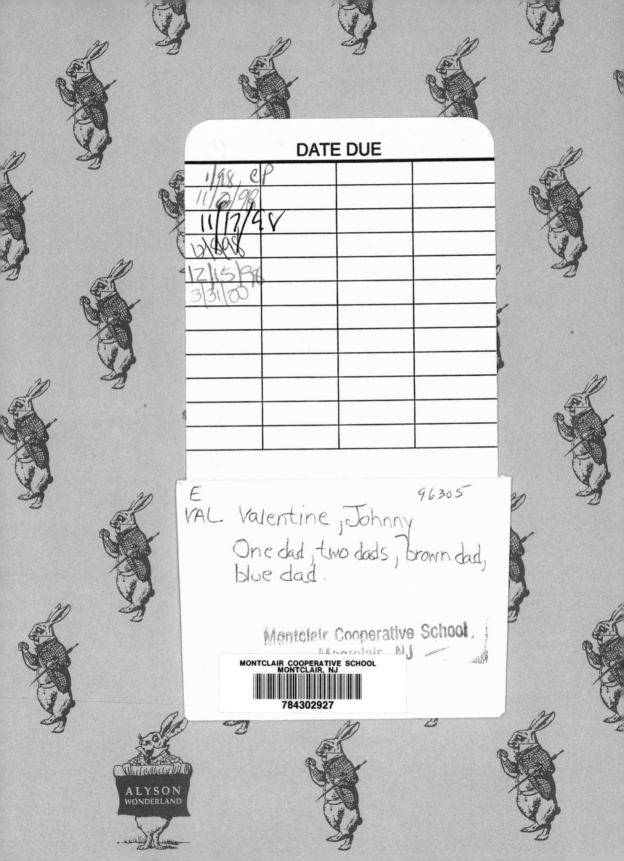

DATE DUE

1/28, CP		
11/2/98		
11/17/98		
12/8/98		
12/15/99		
3/31/00		

E
VAL Valentine, Johnny

96305

One dad, two dads, brown dad,
blue dad.

Montclair Cooperative School,
Montclair, NJ

ALYSON
WONDERLAND